WALT DISNEY'S Pinocchio

Story adapted by Steffi Fletcher
Illustrated by Al Dempster

Digital scanning and restoration services provided by
Tim Lewis of Disney Publishing Worldwide and Ron Stark of S/R Labs

g A GOLDEN BOOK • NEW YORK

www.randomhouse.com/kids/disney
www.goldenbooks.com
ISBN: 0-7364-2152-1
Printed in the United States of America
First Random House Edition   30 29 28 27

One night, the Evening Star shone down on a tiny village. Only one house still had a light burning, and that was the workshop of Geppetto, the kindly old woodcarver. He was busy carving a little puppet.

"Isn't Pinocchio almost like a real boy?" he chuckled.

Climbing into bed, the old man mumbled, "I wish you *were* a real boy, Pinocchio."

Jiminy Cricket overheard Geppetto's wish. He had seen how kind and gentle the woodcarver was, and he felt sorry because the lonely old man's wish could never come true.

Suddenly a shimmering light filled the room. Then a beautiful lady dressed in shining blue appeared. She raised her wand and said:

"Wake, Pinocchio! Skip and run! Good Geppetto needs a son!" Pinocchio blinked his eyes and raised his wooden arms.

"I can move!" he cried. "I'm a real boy!"

"No," the Blue Fairy said sadly. "You have life, but to become a real boy, you must prove yourself brave, truthful, and unselfish."

And Jiminy Cricket would help.

The next morning, Geppetto couldn't believe his eyes. There was his puppet, laughing and talking and running!

"It's true, Father!" Pinocchio cried. "I'm alive!"

After the initial joy was over, Geppetto said, "But now, Pinocchio, you must go to school. Study hard! Then you'll soon become a real boy!"

Meanwhile, Jiminy Cricket had overslept and now jumped up in a great hurry. He caught up with Pinocchio just as the silly little puppet was walking off with the worst pair of scoundrels in the whole countryside—J. Worthington Foulfellow and Gideon.

The villains convinced Pinocchio that he should forget about school and become an actor.

"But, Pinoke!" cried Jiminy. "What will your father say?"

Pinocchio said, "Father will be proud of me!"

Soon they came to a marionette theater. When its owner, Stromboli, saw Pinocchio, his small, evil eyes glistened. "What a drawing card!" he exclaimed. "A puppet without strings!"

The fox nodded. "And he's yours," he said, smiling greedily and holding out his paw, "for a certain price, of course!"

That night Pinocchio sang and danced. The audience cheered for more. A puppet without strings! It was a miracle!

But when Pinocchio started to head home for the night, Stromboli snarled at him. "You're mine, and you stay here!" And *bang!* Before Pinocchio could resist, he was locked in a birdcage!

"Oh, Jiminy," Pinocchio sobbed, "why didn't I go to school? I'll never see my father again!"

Suddenly the Blue Fairy appeared before the sad friends.

"I'll help you this time," she said, "because you are truly sorry. Run home now, Pinocchio, and be a good son, or you'll never become a real boy!"

"Whew!" Pinocchio sighed thankfully. "Let's go home!"

He and Jiminy started running as fast as they could, but whom should they bump into but Foulfellow and Gideon!

This time Foulfellow persuaded the gullible puppet to forget his good resolutions and take a "rest cure" on Pleasure Island.

"You promised to go right home!" Jiminy cried.

"But Foulfellow says I need a rest after my terrible experience."

They came to a coach bound for Pleasure Island. It was pulled by small donkeys and filled with noisy boys. As Pinocchio climbed aboard, Jiminy saw the evil-looking coachman slip Foulfellow a heavy bag. Again the fox had sold Pinocchio!

After boarding a ferry, the coach docked at Pleasure Island. Here streets were paved with cookies, and fountains spouted lemonade.

Pinocchio soon made friends with a young bully called Lampwick who was always in the middle of mischief.

Jiminy was not happy. He shouted at the puppet to go home.

"Don't tell me you're scared of a beetle!" Lampwick snickered.

Jiminy was about to march off when all of a sudden Lampwick and Pinocchio groaned.

The boys were sprouting donkey ears!

"It's donkey fever," whispered Jiminy, horrified. "You were lazy, good-for-nothing boys, so you're turning into donkeys!"

They quickly dashed through the streets.

As they rounded a corner, they saw the coachman herding a bunch of braying donkeys, many of which still wore boys' hats and shoes.

TO THE SALT MINES

Pinocchio and Jiminy managed to climb up the wall surrounding the island, but Lampwick had already turned into a donkey.

There was nothing they could do. With a lump in his throat, Pinocchio followed Jiminy and dove into the sea to escape.

They had a long, hard journey home. By the time they came to the village, it was winter. They hurried to Geppetto's door and pounded on it. But the house was empty!

Just then a gust of wind blew a piece of paper around the corner. "Hey, Pinoke!" Jiminy exclaimed. "It's a letter!"

Dear Pinocchio,

I heard you had gone to Pleasure Island, so Figaro, Cleo, and I started off in a small boat to find you. Just as we came in sight of the island, out of the sea rose Monstro, the giant whale. He opened his jaws; in we went. Now, dear son, we are living in the belly of the whale. But there is very little to eat here, and we cannot exist much longer, so I fear you will never again see

Your loving father,
Geppetto

For a while, they were both silent, too sad to speak. Then Pinocchio stood tall and said, "I am going to save my father!"

Just then a dove wearing a golden crown appeared. "I will take you," she said. "Climb on." Then she spread her wings and flew and flew until they reached the seashore.

Pinocchio and Jiminy did not know that the dove was the Blue Fairy in disguise, and that it was she who had brought them Geppetto's letter.

When the dove was out of sight, Pinocchio tied a big stone to his donkey tail. Then he and Jiminy leaped off the cliff into the ocean below.

As soon as they reached the sandy bottom, Pinocchio scrambled to his feet. "Come on," he said. "Let's find Monstro."

"We'll never find him," muttered Jiminy. "We're probably looking in the wrong ocean!"

Jiminy was wrong. Very near them floated the whale they were looking for, fast asleep. Inside the whale was Geppetto. He had set up a crude home from the ships the whale had swallowed, and every day he fished in the whale's belly. But now that Monstro was sleeping, no fish came in.

"Not a bite for days, Figaro," Geppetto said mournfully to his cat. "If Monstro doesn't wake soon, we'll all starve."

Just then Geppetto felt a nibble. "Food, Figaro!" he cried. But when the catch was landed, it was only a cookbook called *How to Cook Fish.*

It was a solemn moment. All felt that the end was near.

And then the whale moved!

Monstro gave an upward lunge, and through his jaws rushed a wall of water. With it came fish—a whole school of tuna!

Pinocchio saw Monstro coming at him. He held on to a fish and was eaten, too.

Soon Geppetto was pulling fish after fish out of the water. He was so busy, he almost didn't notice Pinocchio getting pulled on board.

"Oh, my own dear son!" he exclaimed. "Is it really you?"

They were thrilled to see each other again. Now if they could only get out of the whale!

Pinocchio had a plan.

The puppet set fire to a pile of crates. As the
fire began to smoke, they jumped onto a raft.
Soon the whale gave a monstrous SNEEZE!

Out went the raft, past those crunching jaws,
into the open sea!

But they were not yet free. The angry whale
plunged after them and splintered their frail craft.

Geppetto was sinking. "My son, save
yourself!" he cried.

But the brave puppet kept him afloat as giant
waves swept them toward the shore.

Geppetto lay on the beach, gratitude filling his
heart. And then he saw Pinocchio lying beside him,
still, cold, and pale! The old man was heartbroken.

Geppetto gathered poor Pinocchio into his arms and headed home. Then he prayed.

Suddenly a ray of starlight appeared. A soft voice said, ". . . And someday, when you have proven yourself brave, truthful, and unselfish, you will be a real boy. . . ."

Pinocchio sat up. He looked at himself and felt his arms and legs. Then he knew!

"Father! Look at me!" he cried joyfully.

The Blue Fairy's promise had come true! Pinocchio was a real, live boy!